Dirty Bertie

My Book of Stuff

STRIPES PUBLISHING
An imprint of Magi Publications
1 The Coda Centre, 189 Munster Road,
London SW6 6AW

A paperback original
First published in Great Britain in 2008

Characters created by David Roberts
Puzzles copyright © Amanda Li, 2008
Text copyright © Amanda Li and Alan MacDonald, 2008
Illustrations copyright © David Roberts, 2008

ISBN: 978-1-84715-049-3

The right of Amanda Li and Alan MacDonald to
be identified as the authors and David Roberts as the
illustrator of this work has been asserted by them in
accordance with the Copyright, Designs and
Patents Act, 1988.

Printed and bound in Belgium

10 9 8 7 6 5 4 3 2 1

DAVID ROBERTS

WRITTEN BY **AMANDA LI** AND **ALAN MACDONALD**

Dirty Bertie

My Book of Stuff

Stripes

I really like doing puzzles, mazes and dot-to-dots, but I've never found any that were about the kinds of things I like. So I thought why not make up my own book – all about me? I spent hours in my bedroom (and used up all Suzy's pens and paper) creating these stink-tastic activities – including favourite things like Whiffer, rubbish, stinkbombs, bogeys and burps, as well as a few unfavourite things like baths, manners and know-All Nick...

So here it is – my very own activity book. I hope you have as much fun doing it as I had making it!

Your friend,

Dirty Bertie

P.S. If you find yourself scratching your head while you're doing this book, it'll be because some of the puzzles are quite tricky. Either that or you've got nits again.

P.P.S. If you get really, really stuck the answers start on page 85!

CLEAN BERTIE/DIRTY BERTIE

Eurgh! My mum's just forced me to get into the bath (I only had one a week ago!) and now I'm sparkling clean. Please can you make me dirty again? Browns, greys and blacks are good colours to use. Let's get grimy!

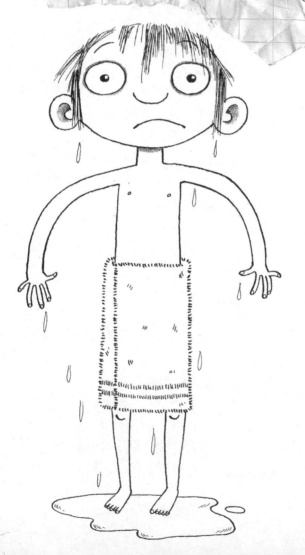

WHOSE TRUMP?
Poo! Which of us has made this nasty niff? Follow the smell trails to find out – but make sure you hold your nose first!

Eugene

Know-All Nick

Bertie

ODD ONE OUT

Look carefully at these five sets of pictures. One picture in each row is not the same as the others. Can you find it and circle it?

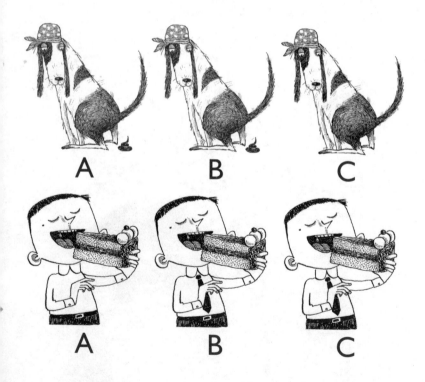

A   B   C

A   B   C

MY BOOK OF STUFF

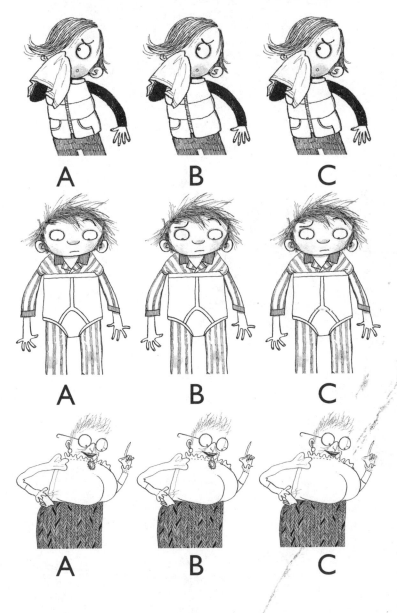

A   B   C

A   B   C

A   B   C

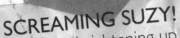

SCREAMING SUZY!
Tee hee! I've been brightening up bedtime by placing some of my favourite creatures under Suzy's duvet! Can you unscramble the creatures' names on the opposite page?

My Book of Stuff

1. sumoe =

2. rowm =

3. lanis =

4. drailz =

5. derips =

6. grof =

BLEEUGH!

Here are some of the things – and people – that make me go 'Bleeugh'! Read my cunning clues opposite and try completing this crossword.

12

My Book of Stuff

Across

1. She's Suzy's friend – and she's also one of my least favourite people in the world. If you've never met her before, here's a clue: what rings at the end of playtime?
3. Why do teachers give out so much of this? Don't we do enough work at school?
4. This is my second worst vegetable. It's green and leafy, and when the school cook boils it up, it stinks to high heaven!
5. Mum makes me wash my face with this stuff – it always gets in my eyes and makes them sting.
6. My most-hated colour. Funnily enough, girls seem to love it.

Down

1. I'm forced to get into one of these every week, which is **much** too often. And when I get out, the water's usually black…
2. My **very worst** vegetable of all-time. It's bright green, sort of flowery with a thick stalk …, euch, I'm feeling sick just thinking about it. It's also difficult to spell, so I'll let you into a secret – it's got a double 'c' in the middle.

ONE, TWO, FLEA!
Scratch, scratch! Good old Whiffer's got fleas again! Can you join the fleas from 1 to 20 to find out what he's dreaming about?

My Book of Stuff

WHY IT WOULD BE GREAT TO BE WHIFFER FOR A DAY

Whiffer's so lucky! It's much better being a dog than a human. Here's why…

No one bats an eyelid when you shove your nose into a pile of rotting rubbish in the street. Or sniff another dog's bottom.

You can growl at people you don't like. Especially Mr Grouch.

Nobody ever asks you the seven times table or to write an essay entitled 'What I did in my school holidays'.

You can go to the park and have a wee up a tree whenever you feel like it.

You can chase the dustcart down the road every week.

You're not expected to say 'Sorry' or 'Excuse me' if you let off a pongy parp. You can just stare at your bottom as if you're really, really surprised.

15

NAME THAT PET

I'd love to have loads of pets, but Mum and Dad aren't so keen. Here are lots of pets I'd like to own – can you think of good names for them? There's just one catch – each name must begin with the same letter as the animal!

Lily _____ lizard

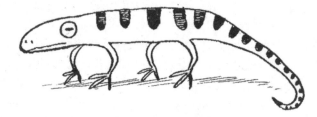

_____ hamster

_____ toad

16

My Book of Stuff

_____ rat

_____ mouse

_____ spider

_____ snake

_____ flea

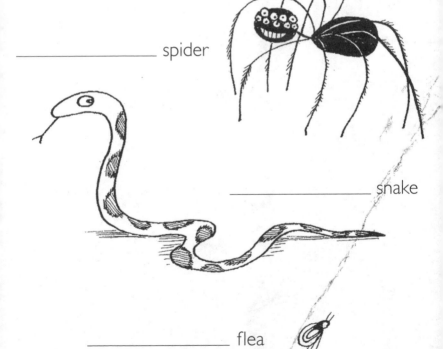

BERTIE'S SECRET CONFESSION

I have a top-secret confession to make to my sister Suzy – but you can only read it if you crack my cunning code. Look at the pictures below and the letters that they represent. Then write the correct letters in the spaces opposite. Tee hee!

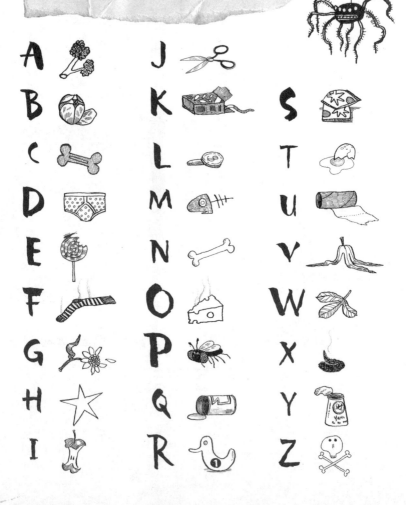

My Book of Stuff

_____

_____

_____

_____

_____

_____

Bertie

WARDROBE WORDSEARCH

Actually, none of these clothes are in my wardrobe – they're all lying on my bedroom floor where I left them last night! Can you find all my clothes in the wordsearch opposite? The words may be backwards, forwards or even diagonal.

TRAINERS

SHORTS

COAT

SHIRT

SHOES

JACKET

PANTS

SOCKS

VEST

TROUSERS

MY BOOK OF STUFF

T	C	A	K	J	A	C	K	E	T
I	T	R	O	U	S	E	R	S	O
R	S	K	N	I	U	V	E	N	H
S	E	R	E	T	E	O	T	E	A
A	V	S	P	E	H	I	U	R	P
S	U	H	E	S	O	C	K	S	H
T	A	O	C	R	N	S	C	H	T
N	C	R	E	C	K	E	U	I	R
A	O	T	R	A	I	N	E	R	S
P	V	S	O	T	S	P	A	T	E

21

ROOTING IN THE RUBBISH

Oh, the sweet smell of rotting vegetables!
Here I am rooting around at my local
rubbish dump, one of my favourite places.
There's lots of great stuff here, but how
many objects can you find that begin
with the letter 'S'?

BIN BRAINSTORMER

There's nothing I like better than investigating a wheelie bin — it may be a bit stinky, but there's so much interesting stuff in there! Can you count how many bins there are in this picture? It's 'wheelie' tricky!

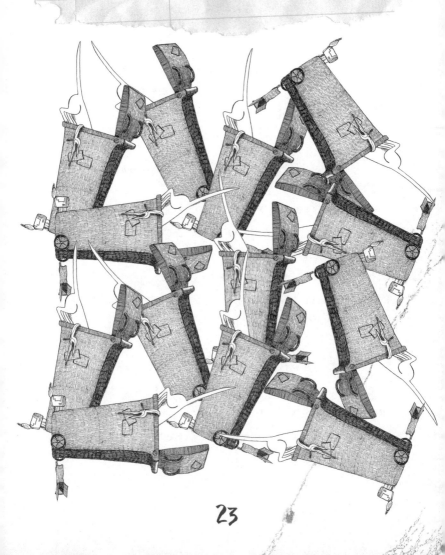

BERTIE'S GROSS TOUCHY-FEELY GAME

This is a brilliant game to play at parties as it gets everyone shuddering and screaming!

You will need:
A grown-up helper
Some large cardboard boxes
Scissors
Several bowls
Yucky things to touch (see list opposite)

① Place the boxes upside down on the floor.

② Cut a hole in one side of each box just big enough to fit your arm through.

③ Place different ingredients in the bowls, and put them inside the boxes so that each bowl can be reached through a hole, but not seen.

④ In turn, ask your friends to put an arm inside the hole and feel what's in the bowl. As they do this, you describe what they are touching, e.g. 'You are now touching real eyeballs!' Or you can write on the outside of the box what each hole contains, e.g. worms!

Yucky things to put in the bowls:

Peeled grapes or olives – eyeballs
Cold spaghetti or noodles – worms
Little sausages or carrots – cut-off fingers
Slime – snot
Balls of play dough – poo
Fake fur – a dead animal
Breadsticks – broken bones
Hard-boiled eggs (without shells) – hearts
Uncooked popcorn – teeth
Jelly – brains or guts
Insects – toy plastic insects such as spiders

If you don't have cardboard boxes, you can play
this game by getting everyone to sit on the floor
in a circle and turning the lights out. Then you
pass each bowl around the circle while describing
the gruesome contents. You will hear lots of
'Euurghs' and 'Yucks' as your friends touch the
disgusting items!

Tee hee! Here's a picture of me and my family. Mum told me off for pulling a silly face. Can you spot nine differences in the second picture opposite?

MY BOOK OF STUFF

LEAF IT OUT!

Watch out! Mr Grouch is sweeping up leaves and they're going everywhere! Look carefully among the leaves and see if you can identify seven things. Then write them in the giant leaf opposite.

I can see…

30

JOIN THE DOTS
Join the dots to find out what I'm dreaming about. Hmmm…

WIGGLING WORDSNAKE

I love going into the garden and finding new bugs for my creepy-crawly collection! Here are some of my favourite ones. Can you trace the words in the grid opposite using a pencil? The words go in one continuous line, snaking up and down, and backwards and forwards, but never diagonally. They are in the same order as the list here. I've done the first word to help you!

SNAIL

BEETLE

CATERPILLAR

S	N	A	F	L
B	L	I	R	Y
E	L	E	E	D
E	T	C	P	I
E	T	A	S	E
R	L	L	E	D
P	I	A	P	I
O	W	R	N	T
R	A	R	E	C
M	E	W	I	G

SCHOOL DINNER MIX-UP

Oh dear! Mrs Mould the dinner lady
has got our school dinners all
muddled. Can you match them up
again by drawing a line between the
correct words?

School dinner

Fish	bolognese
Jacket	crumble
Spaghetti	beans
Rice	nuggets
Apple	potato
Baked	fingers
Chicken	soup
Tomato	pudding

DINNER DILEMMA

Oh no! The new dinner lady, Miss Beansprout, starts today, and she only wants to see healthy food in the school canteen! Can you get rid of all the unhealthy snacks before she arrives? Cross out the pictures below to leave only the healthy food.

VET MUDDLE

Taking Whiffer to the vets was a big mistake. Now all the animals are running around in a crazy mixed-up rumpus! All their names have got mixed up, too. Can you unscramble them?

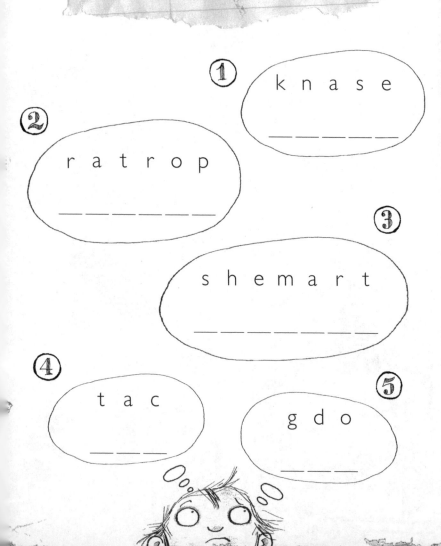

① k n a s e

_ _ _ _ _

② r a t r o p

_ _ _ _ _ _

③ s h e m a r t

_ _ _ _ _ _ _

④ t a c

_ _ _

⑤ g d o

_ _ _

37

BERTIE'S TERRIFYINGLY TASTY TARANTULAS

These creepy-crawly cakes are gruesomely realistic and terrifically tasty to eat. Make sure you lick the spoon when no one's looking. Yummy!

You will need:

A grown-up helper
6 ready-made fairy cakes
(or mini muffins) in paper cases
30g soft butter
50g icing sugar
1 tablespoon drinking chocolate powder
Smarties or chocolate buttons for eyes
A packet of black liquorice laces
Bowl
Wooden spoon
Sieve
Scissors

How to make:

1. First, make the chocolate butter icing. Sift the icing sugar into a bowl so that there are no lumps in it, then sift the drinking chocolate on top of the icing sugar. Mix them together.

2. Add the soft butter and mix it with the wooden spoon until you have a creamy brown icing. Mmmm!

3. Take the first cake and use a teaspoon to cover the entire top of the cake with the yummy icing. This is your spider's body.

4. Cut the liquorice laces up into pieces about 5cm long. Each cake will need eight liquorice legs.

5. To create your spider, place two Smarties, or other round sweets, on the front of the spider for its 'eyes'. Then press eight pieces of liquorice into the icing around the body for its 'legs'. Repeat the procedure for the other cakes.

6. There you have it – a tray of terrifying tarantulas! Eat them as quickly as possible before your friends and family spot them and gobble the lot!

DESIGN MY FANCY DRESS

It's Eugene's birthday party next week and I need a new fancy dress outfit to wear. Can you draw one for me? Bugs, beasts, pirates, aliens, that kind of thing — definitely nothing girly or stinky pinky. OK?

BERTIE'S BEST EXCUSES TO AVOID GIRLS' PARTIES

I love birthday parties — crisps, cake, fizzy drinks, games — brilliant! But girls' parties are a different matter. I was once forced to go to Angela Nicely's party, and not only was it FULL of girls (bleuggh!) but everything was sickly PINK! Double bleuggh! Here's how to avoid a party:

ACT SICK

Pretend that you've caught a serious illness on the morning of the party. For extra effect, rush to the bathroom every five minutes and make loud sick noises. Use Mum's make-up to give yourself a pale sickly appearance.

ACT DUMB

'Lose' the invitation, rub out the word 'party' on the calendar and never mention it again. With any luck, your busy mum and dad won't remember you were supposed to be going to a party at all.

JUST HIDE

Find a really good hiding place (laundry basket, wardrobe, shed, etc.), pack essential supplies of crisps and lemonade and 'disappear' for a while. Ensure that you only emerge WHEN THE PARTY IS OVER — come out too early and you'll be frogmarched to the girly nightmare.

DESPERATE MEASURES

If you're forced to go to the party, make sure you behave so badly that you're never invited back again.

41

MY BIRTHDAY BRAINSTORM

Hurrah! It's my birthday, the best day of the year, and there's so much delicious food and so many fun things to do, I don't know where to start! Can you work out my birthday brainstormers?

1. If I eat four sandwiches, how many will be left?

2. If I scoff two pieces of birthday cake, how many pieces will be left?

42

③ If I open five presents, how many will I have left?

④ If I pop seven balloons, how many will be left?

BOUNCING DOT-TO-DOT

Wheel I'm having a great time at this party! Can you join the numbered dots to find out what I'm bouncing on?

PARTY PUZZLE

I can't wait for my next birthday party! Can you guess what I'm going to dress up as? Look at the pictures below and write the first letter of each word in the correct space to find out.

TROLLEY TRAUMA

Oh no! Gran's been to the butcher's to buy sausages and now Whiffer's made off with her shopping! Can you help her get it back? Trace a path through the maze below.

HOW'S YOUR MEMORY?

I'm not very good at remembering things, especially stuff like homework and tidying my room. How good is your memory? Look at my box of top-secret possessions that I keep under my bed, but for one minute only. Then cover the picture with a piece of paper and see if you can write down six things that were in my box.

CHEWY BIG LUMP

Whoopee

Bertie's Book
Strickly
Private
Keep out

TOP-SECRET
POSSESSIONS

Bogeys

BERTIE'S FAVOURITE THINGS

This is more like it – six of my favourite things! Look at the picture clues and write the words in the correct spaces on the crossword. I've done one letter already to help you! Tip! Count the number of letters in each word to see which space they fit into.

My Book of Stuff

VOWEL VOMIT

Here are some of my favourite words – if you've been reading my books, I'm sure you'll recognize them! Each word has one letter missing. Which vowel – A, E, I, O or U – is the missing letter? Look at the pile of sick below and cross off each vowel as you use it.

sm__ll   b__rp

s__ck   p__rp

b__gey

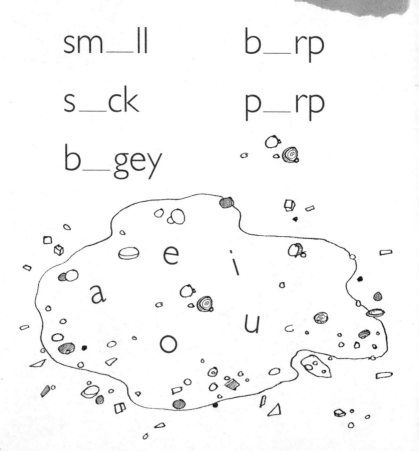

KEEP OUT OF NICK'S WAY!

That Know-All Nick wants to play a trick on me so I'm trying to avoid him. Can you help me get to Whiffer without bumping into him? Trace a pencil line through the maze — but, remember, don't go anywhere near Nasty Nick!

SCHOOL WORDSNAKE

School's OK, I suppose, but it would be a lot better if they sacked all the teachers and let the pupils take over! Then we could do fun stuff like this great wordsnake I've made up. There are 11 school-related words in the grid opposite, in the same order as the list below. Can you trace them, using a pencil? The words go in one continuous line, snaking up and down, forwards and backwards, but never diagonally.

1 PENCIL   2 BAG

3 RULER

4 TEACHER   5 HEAD

6 PLAYGROUND   7 RUBBER

9 BOOK   8 DESK

10 HOMEWORK

11 PEN

P	C	I	R	K	N
E	N	L	O	P	E
G	A	B	W	E	M
R	U	O	K	H	O
E	L	O	B	K	S
R	T	B	R	D	E
R	E	A	E	B	B
H	H	C	D	R	U
E	P	L	N	U	O
A	D	A	Y	G	R

SHADOW MATCH

Eek! You wouldn't want to meet some of the people I know on a dark night! Can you match this scary lot to their shadows?

BERTIE'S BEST WAYS TO ANNOY YOUR TEACHER

These ideas made me laugh, but I wouldn't actually DO any of them. Why? Because I would get into BIG TROUBLE if I did. Like that time when I locked Mr Weakly in a cupboard – though I probably shouldn't have dressed up in his clothes and tried to teach the class as well…

- Pretend you've got an upset stomach and ask to go to the toilet every five minutes.
- Wear Deely Boppers to school and talk in an alien voice all day.
- Lock your teacher in the art cupboard (yes, I know it's been done before) BUT this time, impersonate your headteacher's voice so that he gets the blame.
- Get hold of the PE teacher's whistle and block it up with a piece of chewing gum.
- Ask 'But why?' after every SINGLE statement your teacher makes.
- When your teacher turns to the whiteboard, hide all his/her pens.
- Sniff constantly.
- Let off one of your home-made stinkbombs under the teacher's desk.

MR GROUCH'S WORD LADDER

Oh no, here comes Mr Grouch in his usual grumpy mood. Can you complete each pair of three-letter words by writing one letter inside each rung of his ladder? If you do, you'll find out how Mr Grouch feels whenever he sees me at school! I've done the first one for you.

TE	A	RM
TI		IT
EG		AP
EA		AT
BO		ES

ARTHUR'S NEW HOME

I usually keep my pet earthworm, Arthur, in a goldfish bowl filled with mud, leaves and a plastic soldier for company. But he's getting bored and needs some new surroundings. Can you draw him a worm-tastic new home with a fun play area for him to wriggle around in?

HELP ARTHUR!

Oh no! My pet earthworm, Arthur, has wriggled out of his goldfish bowl and is lost. Can you help him find his way back home? Follow the slimy worm trails to find the right way.

WHICH WHIFFER?

Wow! What a lot of Whiffers there are!
They may seem identical but look very carefully
— one Whiffer is different from the others.
Can you find him?

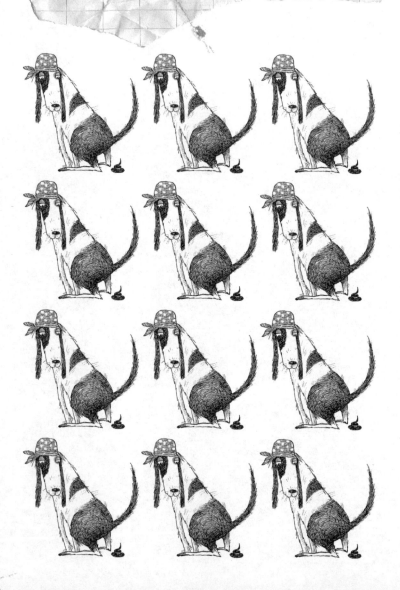

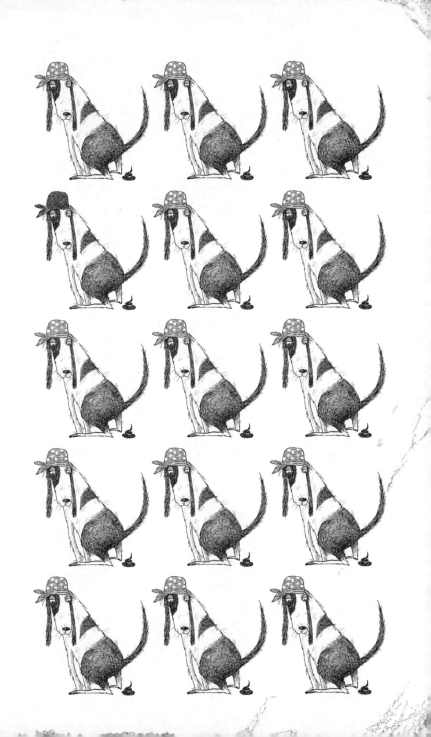

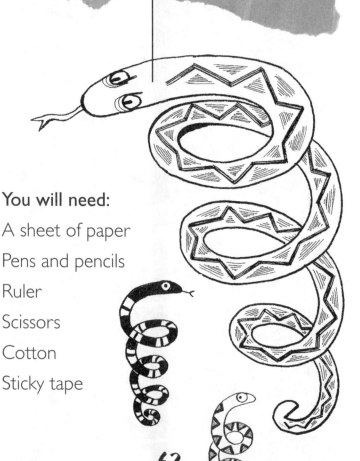

BERTIE'S SCARY SNAKE MAKE

This spiral snake is super-easy to make and will scare off any intruders if you hang it in your bedroom. I make lots in different colours and hang them from a coat hanger to give my big sis a big hiss!

You will need:

A sheet of paper

Pens and pencils

Ruler

Scissors

Cotton

Sticky tape

How to make:

- Cut out a square of paper 15cm x 15cm.
- Draw a spiral snake to fill the square, just like the picture below.
- Draw a pattern on the snake and colour it in with lots of bright colours. Don't forget to add two scary eyes to the head. You could even make a forked tongue out of the spare paper and glue it on for extra effect!
- Cut out the snake in a spiral and stick a length of cotton to the top of the snake's head with the sticky tape. Hang from your ceiling or from a coat hanger. Snakes alive!

BERTIE'S REVOLTING RHYMES

I bet you never guessed I was a poet on the quiet! I like to scribble these little rhymes in my notebook – the more disgusting, the better.
Can you help me by finishing each rhyme with one word from the list at the end?

Look at this! I've never seen
A bogey that's so big and _____.

Achoo! Pass a hanky, please
I'm going to do another _____.

Bertie! What's that on your shirt?
It's only mud and grime and _____.

My Book of Stuff

I like to smell things with my nose
Especially my cheesy _____.

Fizzy drinks are great to slurp
Then afterwards you start to _____.

Does something round here smell,
you think?
Oh no, it's Bertie's socks –
they _____!

SNEEZE

GREEN

BURP

TOES

DIRT

STINK

CREATE A SLIMY SALAD

One of my proudest moments was creating a new salad for school dinners, with a secret 'fresh ingredient' – MAGGOTS! Miss Skinner nearly jumped out of her skin when she tasted the salty squishy flavour!

Can you create a slimy, squishy salad that's even more disgusting than mine? Caterpillars with cucumber? Snails and salad? Why not add some extra crunch with an earwig or two? Mmmm! Draw these on the plate below.

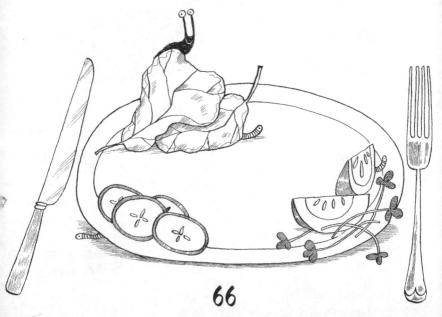

BERTIE'S WORST SMELLS

These are the VERY stinkiest smells I have personally experienced. I would love to sniff a durian fruit, which is supposed to be the worst smell in the world ever. It grows in Asia and has been described as smelling like skunks, vomit and old socks! I wish I could get hold of one and hide it in Mr Grouch's shed!

- My homemade stinkbombs – the best!
- Whiffer's windy bottom, especially when he's been eating leftover cabbage from my plate.
- A full wheelie bin at the end of a hot week. Poo-ee!
- Suzy's stinky horrible perfume – much worse than any dog poo.
- The ham sandwich I left in the outside pocket of my rucksack all summer. When I found it, it was bright green and stank to high heaven!
- Eau de Wet Whiffer. When he's been swimming in the canal and is drying himself in front of the fire, it's best to leave the house for a few days...
- Sick – but only other people's.
- The school toilets, especially when one of us has caused a 'blockage' that Mr Grouch hasn't dealt with.
- My cheesy trainers. Mum makes me leave them outside the back door as she says the smell is 'deathly'. That makes me so proud!

Bertie's Super-smelly STINKBOMB - Mark ①

1 lump of pongy cheese   1 sweaty football sock
4 rotten eggs   3 mouldy cabbage leaves
1 tin of dogfood   Dog hairs - a goodhandful

WORLD'S SMELLIEST STINKBOMB

I spent weeks collecting the most pongy ingredients I could find for my special stinkbomb – and, believe me, it really reeked! If you were making a stinkbomb, what smelly ingredients would you put in it? Write your rancid recipe below.

My own Super-smelly Stinkbomb

1. THE BLUEBOTTLE
AT THE BARBECUE

I once pretended that a fly was buzzing around during a family barbecue and made a big fuss about flapping it away and trying to swat it. When no one was looking, I took out a raisin that I already had hidden in my pocket. Then I announced to everyone that I'd caught the fly, quickly showed them the raisin and then popped it in my mouth! You should have seen their faces as I chewed away! Gran nearly choked on her burger and Suzy ran out of the garden screaming. What a result!

2. TIME FOR A CHANGE

Mum, Dad and Suzy didn't see the funny side when I changed ALL the clocks in the house (apart from mine, of course) so that they were an hour fast. You should have seen them on Monday morning, rushing around and shouting, thinking that they were really late! Then they all arrived at work and school before either of them were open! Mind you, Mum and Dad got their own back on me that evening when I was sent to bed TWO WHOLE HOURS early…
How unfair is that?

3. POO TO YOU

Know-All Nick really deserved this one after all the mean tricks he's played on me in the past! At home I prepared some realistic-looking 'poo' using a large piece of brown play dough. It looked really convincing after I had worked on it for a while with my modelling tools. The next day, I got into school early and put the 'poo' under Know-All Nick's chair. When class started, I began to sniff loudly, saying, "Poo, what's that terrible smell?" Looking around, I pointed to Nick's chair and said, "Look everyone, I don't think Nick made it to the toilet in time!" You should have seen his red face as he tried to deny it!

PUZZLING PAWPRINTS

Whiffer's tummy's rumbling and he wants his dinner. Can you fill in the missing numbers to lead him to his bowl? Look carefully at the number sequence below.

BERTIE'S BEST WAYS TO GET REALLY, REALLY DIRTY

- Accidentally fall into a ditch or a canal. You not only get dirty, but wet and smelly, too! Three for the price of one – excellent!
- Audition for the role of the chimney sweep in the musical 'Mary Poppins'.
- Go to your local farm and roll around with the pigs.
- Slip in one of Whiffer's big poos.
- Explore your local rubbish dump wearing a white T-shirt and trousers.
- Empty a bucket of coal on your head.
- Play football on a waterlogged field. Mum's face will be a picture when you present her with your muddy kit.
- Get creative in an art activity involving a lot of black paint.
- Become a part-time dustman. Brilliant!
- Go to a farm and stand under an cow's bottom just as he lifts his tail…

SPOT THE DIFFERENCE
As usual, Dad's managing to drive the car
and tell me off at the same time ...
humph! Can you spot seven differences
in the picture opposite?

MY BOOK OF Stuff

COLOURFUL CLUES

Read each of my clues to guess the colour. Then find the colour in the wordsearch opposite – it could be backwards, forwards or diagonal.

1. The colour of snot and bogeys. And also broccoli.
2. One of my favourite colours – the colour of coal, ink and vampires' cloaks. Also the colour of my ears, Mum says, when they haven't been washed for a while.
3. Yeeuch! I hate this colour – it's the most girly, yukky, stupid colour in the world. Think fairies, ballet skirts … I can't go on!
4. My fly, Buzz, is a ——bottle.
5. The colour of school custard.
6. A great colour – think mud and grime!
7. When I fall over and bruise myself this is the colour the bruise goes. Also the colour of plums.
8. The colour of blood.

76

B	A	R	B	L	A	C	K	C
L	S	G	R	E	E	N	D	A
O	R	N	O	P	F	I	C	U
G	O	S	W	O	L	L	E	Y
W	K	D	N	I	Y	H	W	N
E	I	A	M	R	K	K	T	A
U	F	P	E	L	N	C	K	C
L	T	D	R	I	L	U	M	O
B	E	W	P	U	R	P	L	E

JUST HOW DIRTY ARE YOU?

Tick a, b, or c to find out if you're a proper Dirty Bertie, a slightly-grubby Eugene or a sparkling Suzy.

1. What colour is the water after you've had a bath?

a. It's just as clean as when you first got in!

b. A bit greyish with a touch of scum floating on the top.

c. Completely black with a few bugs swimming around in it.

2. You're about to sneeze - and it's going to be a big one! What do you do?

a. Use a crisp new tissue (you always have one in your pocket) to catch the sneeze, while saying 'Bless me!'

b. Try to find a tissue, fail, and use your sleeve instead.

c. Wait till you've sneezed, then use your hand to wipe off the snot, smearing it all across your face.

Inspect any big bogeys clinging to the back of your hand.

3. How would you describe the state of your bedroom?

a. A haven of sweet-scented peace and calm where everything is clean, tidy and ordered alphabetically.

b. Fairly untidy, a little dusty, but not a bad place for a sleepover.

c. You're not sure what your bedroom actually looks like - there's so much stuff everywhere you haven't seen it in years!

4. How often do you wash your face?

a. Every morning and evening, of course! You would never forget.

b. Most nights before bedtime, if you remember.

c. Only when your parents notice how dirty your face is and you are forced into the bathroom. Luckily, this doesn't happen very often.

5. You discover a forgotten yoghurt lurking in the back of the fridge. It's half-open, has green mould sprouting out of

the top and stinks of old socks and cheese. What's your first reaction?

a. You nearly throw up at the sight and chuck the revolting thing straight into the bin - making sure you first put on protective plastic gloves.

b. You're slightly shocked, but also interested in having a good look at the gruesome growths with a magnifying glass.

c. What a great find! And it will make a fascinating addition to the stinking collection of objects you keep underneath your bed.

6. What's you worst habbit?

a. You hate to admit it, but on some busy mornings you forget to polish your shoes before you leave the house.

b. Well, you can be a bit windy at times, but you do try to keep your stinkiest farts for the privacy of your bedroom.

c. Mmmm, tricky - you've got so many - picking your nose and eating the contents, burping loudly at the table, never flushing the loo when you've done a poo - take your pick!

How did you score?

Mostly As
What a sparkling Suzy you are!
Everything about you is super-
clean, from your gleaming teeth
to your immaculate white socks.
How do you do it, you Queen of
Clean?

Mostly Bs
You're a very average slightly-
grubby Eugene. Being clean
doesn't come naturally to you, but
you do remember to wash your face
and brush your teeth now and
again. But you also enjoy getting
down and dirty when someone like
Bertie's around!

Mostly Cs
You and Dirty Bertie must be
twins - we reckon you're partners
in grime! You just can't seem to
help attracting dust and dirt
wherever you are, and you have so
many disgusting habits we
couldn't begin to count them. You
really are the Master of Muck!

That's all for now!

Unless you're Know-All Nick and know EVERYTHING, you might find the next few pages handy — it's the answers!

Answers!

Pg 7: It's Eugene – poo!

Pg 8–9: C, A, B, A, C

Pg 10–11: 1. mouse, 2. worm, 3. snail, 4. lizard, 5. spider, 6. frog

Pg 12: Your crossword should look like this:

¹B	E	L	L	A					
A									
T				²B					
³H	O	M	E	W	O	R	K		
				R					
				O					
				⁴C	A	B	B	A	G	E
				C					
			⁵S	O	A	P			
				L					
			⁶P	I	N	K			

Pg 14: A bone!

Pg 18–19: Secret code reads: I put a hairy spider in your school bag!

Pg 21: It should look like this:

Pg 22: Saw, squirrel, sausages, spoon, spider, shoe, scissors, skipping rope, spade

Pg 23: There are 13 wheelie bins. Stinky!

Pg 26–27: The differences are:

    1. Dad's beard is missing

    2. Dad's looking in a different direction

    3. Bertie's not sticking his tongue out

    4. Mum's beauty spot is missing

    5. Cat's tail is missing

    6. Whiffer's whiskers are missing

    7. Suzy's dress is different

    8. Mum's looking in a different direction

    9. Suzy's nose is missing!

Pg 28–29: The hidden things are:

    1. Bertie

    2. a ladder

    3. a frog

    4. a bike

    5. a poo

    6. a satchel

    7. a cat

Pg 31: It's Whiffer!

Pg 33: It should look like this:

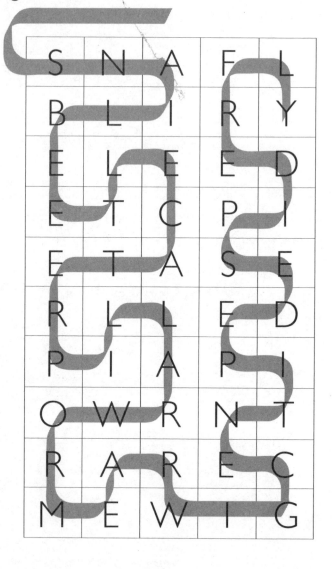

Pg 34: The school dinners should be:

Fish fingers

Jacket potato

Spaghetti bolognese

Rice pudding

Apple crumble

Baked beans

Chicken nuggets

Tomato soup

Pg 35: The food left behind should be: banana, avocado, carrot, apple, pepper, strawberries and broccoli.

Pg 36: The animals are:

1. Snake, 2. Parrot, 3. Hamster, 4. Cat, 5. Dog

Pg 42–43:

1. Five

2. Six

3. Two

4. Four

Pg 44: A bouncy castle!

Pg 45: A pirate!

Pg 46: Your maze should look like this:

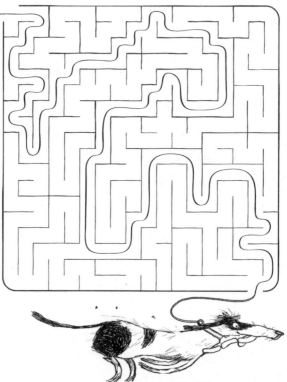

Pg 48–49: Your crossword should look like this:

Pg 50: The words should be: smell, burp, sick, parp, bogey

Pg 51: Your maze should look like this:

Pg 53: Your wordsnake should look like this:

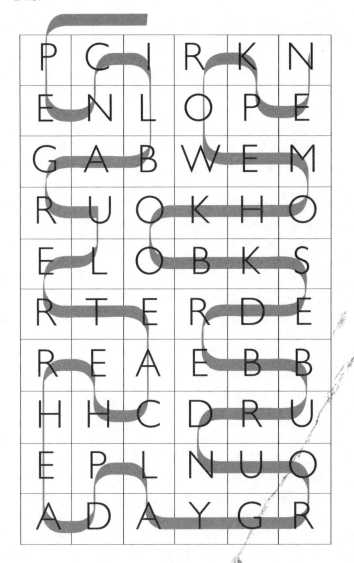

Pg 54–55: 1. C, 2. D, 3. A, 4. B

Pg 57: Mr Grouch feels ANGRY!

Pg 59: The correct trail is C.

Pg 60–61: The first Whiffer on the sixth row has a different pirate hat!

Pg 64–65: Bertie's Revolting Rhymes:

Look at this! I've never seen
A bogey that's so big and **green**.
Achoo! Pass a hanky, please
I'm going to do another **sneeze**.
Bertie! What's that on your shirt?
It's only mud and grime and **dirt**.
I like to smell things with my nose
Especially my cheesy **toes**.
Fizzy drinks are great to slurp
Then afterwards you start to **burp**.
Does something round here smell, you think?
Oh no, it's Bertie's socks – they **stink**!

Pg 72: The missing numbers are: 16, 20, 28, 32, 40, 44 and 52.

Pg 74: 1. Dad's hair is different, 2. The tax disc is missing on the windscreen,

3. Bertie's looking in a different direction,
4. The wing mirror has changed position,
5. Bertie is smiling, 6. Whiffer is sitting up!
7. The rear-view mirror is missing.

Page 76–77. Your wordsearch should look like this:

Pg 78–79:

Suzy says: "You are the stinkiest little brother in the whole world!"

Mum says: "Please go and tidy your bedroom, Bertie!"

Whiffer says: "Woof, woof!"

Gran says: "Have you been playing with my teeth, Bertie?"

Miss Boot says: "Bertie! No running in the school corridor!"